# The Gwibber

Written by Lisa Thompson
Pictures by Luke Jurevicius and Arthur Moody

Gog was excited.

"Come quickly!" he yelled to Binks the elf.
"I want to show you something special."

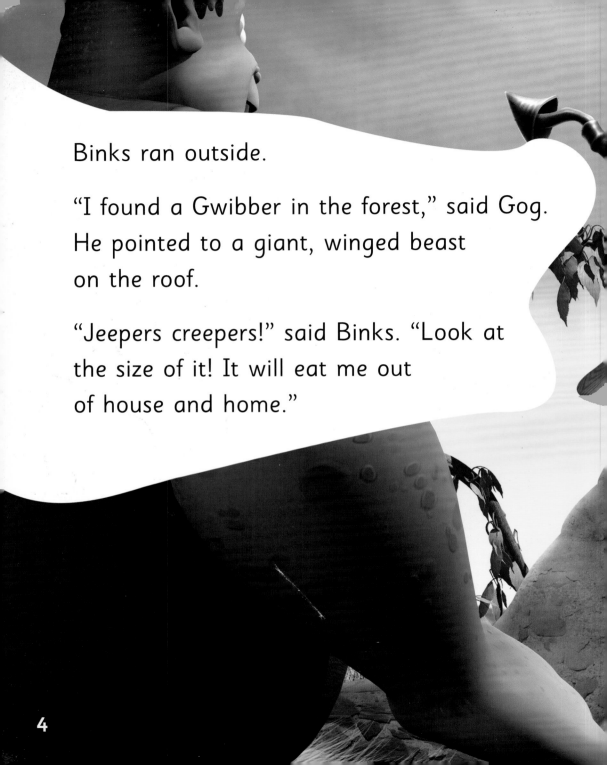

Binks ran outside.

"I found a Gwibber in the forest," said Gog. He pointed to a giant, winged beast on the roof.

"Jeepers creepers!" said Binks. "Look at the size of it! It will eat me out of house and home."

"This Gwibber will be a great guard dog," said Gog.

"You are a giant. You don't need a guard dog!" said Binks.

6

The Gwibber flew off the roof.
He was hungry, so he looked
around for something to eat.
He spotted the vegetable patch.

"Bother!" said Binks.
"All my beans have gone."

Now the Gwibber was thirsty.
He looked all around him,
trying to find something to drink.
Then he spotted the fish pond.

"Jumping jellybeans!" said Binks.
"All my water has gone."

Next the Gwibber walked to the fence.
He was tired, so he looked around
for a good place to sleep.
He dug a hole in the garden.

"Jeepers creepers!" said Binks.
"My garden has gone!"

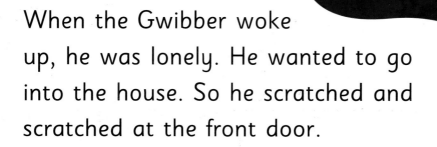

When the Gwibber woke up, he was lonely. He wanted to go into the house. So he scratched and scratched at the front door.

"Galloping goblins!" said Binks. "Now my front door has gone!"

The Gwibber was still hungry,
so he sniffed and snuffled
all around the house.
He found the place where Binks
hid her chocolate biscuits.

"Jumping jellybeans!" said Binks.
"All my chocolate biscuits have gone!"

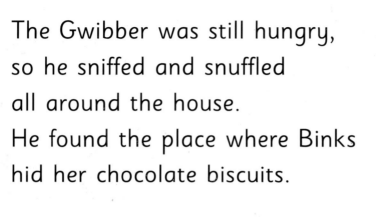

That night, the Gwibber could not sleep.
He screeched and howled all night long.

"Bother!" said Binks. "I need my sleep!
I'm sick and tired of that Gwibber!"

19

Binks ran off into the forest.
She screeched and howled, and she made all kinds of Gwibber noises.

Gog's Gwibber heard the noises.
"Great!" he said. "I can hear some other Gwibbers!"
He flew off to find them.

SCREECH!

SQUAWK!

"Jeepers creepers!" said Binks. "That's wonderful! The Gwibber has gone!" Binks climbed back into bed and fell fast asleep.

"I'm really going to miss that Gwibber," said Gog.